CHESTER'S EASIEST PIANO COUR

Book 3

by Carol Barratt

with illustrations by Sarah Lenton

Chester Music

(A division of Music Sales Ltd.)
8/9 Frith Street, London W1V 5TZ
Exclusive distributors: Music Sales Ltd., Newmarket Road, Bury St. Edmunds, Suffolk, IP33 3YB

This book belongs to ....

CH 55973

Teachers and Parents

This comprehensive Piano Course, in three books, can be used by the youngest beginner. Various games and puzzles are included to help the pupil absorb the information by having fun at the same time.

To reinforce certain topics, suggestions for supplementary material – drawn from Chester Piano Teaching Material – have been added in italics at the bottom of certain pages. For Book 3 of this course, supplementary material has been drawn from the following books:

Chester's Music Puzzles Set Two (CH 55832)/ **Chester's Piano Starters Volume Two** (CH 55662)

Warm Up With Chester Part One (CH 55768)

Move on fairly quickly as the pieces should be well within the pupil's capabilities.

Enjoy yourselves!

Carol Barratt

Hello – it's me again, Chester Junior.

Let's get started on Book Three – I can't wait !

Watch out for the rest of the gang – Mo, Bradley, Lizzie and Eric. (My famous Dad, Chester, appears in the supplementary books).

sigh

and

INK

4

CHESTER'S CHART
HINTS AND REMINDERS

1. Listen as you play.

2. Hold your fingers in a curved shape and play on the tips of your fingers — as if you were holding a very small orange in each hand. Your hand is a bridge which mustn't collapse.

3. Your wrists should be level with your arms.

4. **Don't** look down at your hands.

5. Look at the **shape** of the music on the page (for **Steps**, **Skips** and **Jumps**) before you play.

6. **Always** practise with the correct fingering.

7. Practise hands separately. When each part is perfect, try it hands together **slowly**. You can always play the pieces faster when you really know them.

Mo's Chart
i) Feed the Cat.

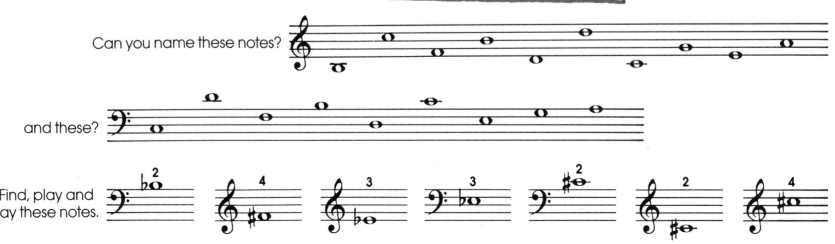

Can you name these notes?

and these?

Find, play and say these notes.

THREE CHEERS FOR CHESTER!

C.B.

Allegro

f

* In this book the finger numbers are no longer in circles.

STEPS, SKIPS AND JUMPS

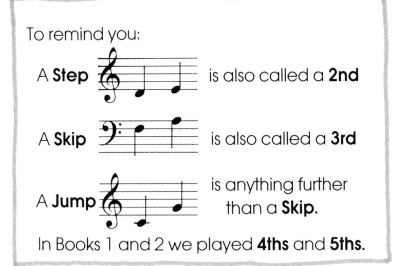

To remind you:

A **Step** is also called a **2nd**

A **Skip** is also called a **3rd**

A **Jump** is anything further than a **Skip**.

In Books 1 and 2 we played **4ths** and **5ths**.

Play these **Jumps**.
Are they **4ths** or **5ths**?

Play some **Skips** anywhere on the Piano.

Play **Octave Jumps** anywhere on the Piano.

Copy them into your Manuscript Book, writing the letter-names underneath, and naming the **Jumps** like this.

5th
C   G

Warm-up

OLD GERMAN DANCE

What is the name of the Key Signature?

Adapted from
Michael Praetorius (1571–1621)

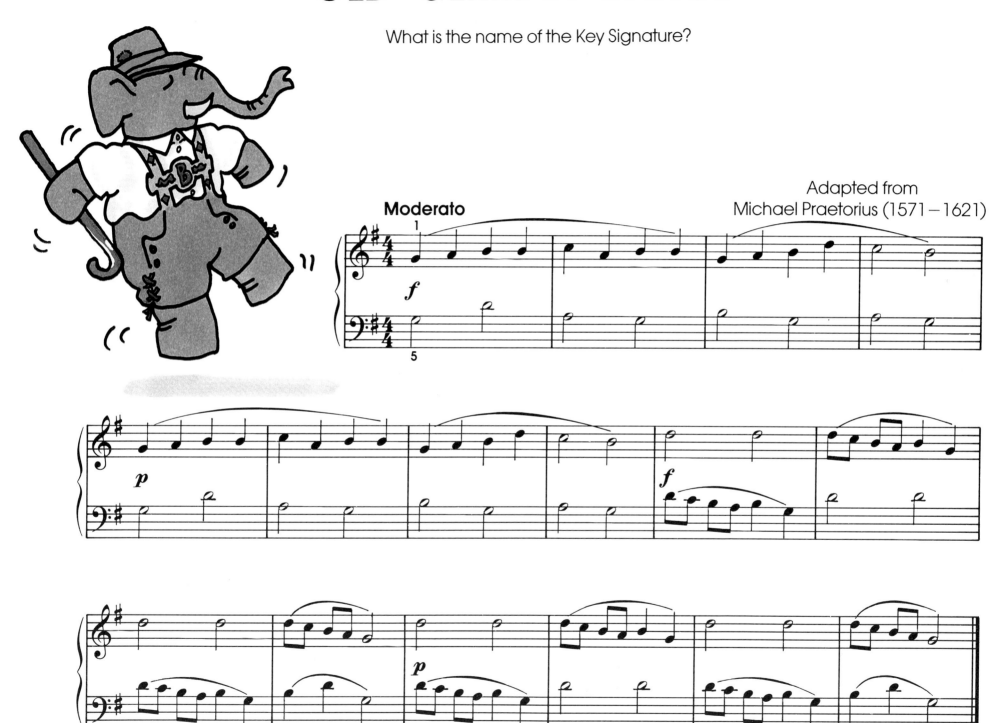

Supplementary material: Chester's Music Puzzles Set Two, paper 6.

IN THE HAMMOCK

rit. (ritenuto) = Slow down

Watch out — the tune is in the Left Hand.

Slowly swinging

Adapted from a Hungarian Folk Tune

PAUSE FOR PAWS!

⌢ = **Pause**. When you have played the note with ⌢ above it,
say "Pause" in your head before moving on or ending the piece.

Try playing the Right Hand an Octave higher than it is written.

TURKEY IN THE STRAW

American Traditional

OVER THE HILLS AND FAR AWAY

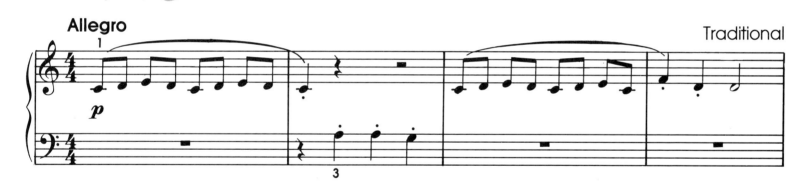

Allegro

Traditional

Supplementary material: Chester's Piano Starters Volume Two, p.7.

NEW POSITION — OLD NOTES

Put 1 of your  on the **F** above **Middle C**.

F G A B♭ C

Practise writing and naming these notes in your Manuscript Book using Steps, Skips and Jumps.

HUMMING SONG

What is the name of the Key Signature?

Adapted from
Robert Schumann (1810—1856)

Moderato

When you can play this piece, see if you can hum it!

RISE AND SHINE!

This piece is in the Key of **F** Major. Czerny originally wrote it
in **C** Major and called it *Staccato Study.*

Carl Czerny (1791 – 1857)

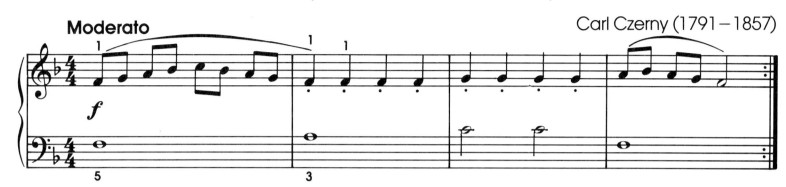

Wake up your Left Hand by playing the Right Hand tune above

starting on and so on.

Supplementary material: Warm Up With Chester Part One, p.18. Chester's Music Puzzles Set Two, paper 7.

TIME TO WRITE

...a B pencil, how nice...

Remember, use a B or 2B pencil.

1. Write the notes as ♩s for each letter-name given.

A   F♯   Middle B   E♭   E   Middle D   B♭   G♯

2. Add Bar Lines and a Double Bar Line to this piece, then complete the counts.
   Put ( ) round the Rest counts.

3   +   4   +

one of them must be right...

3. Play each tune below and add the note you think it should end on.
   Write this last note in the last Bar. This note will be the **Key-note** and gives you the name of the Key.
   (To make it more difficult, the Key Signatures have been left out and ♯s and ♭s added to notes.)

?

Key of . . . . .

?

Key of . . . . .

CRASH!!

BRADLEY'S SOB—STORY

BRAVE KNIGHT

Look carefully at the ✋ position before you start:

Mini Warm-up

B C D E F Two new notes

Like a March

Moritz Vogel (1846–1922)

Supplementary material: Chester's Piano Starters Volume Two, p.8.

QUIET TIME

Look carefully at the hand positions before you start:

This piece is in a **Minor** Key (**E** Minor). Major and Minor Scales and Keys are looked at in later books.

E F# G A B

E F# G A B

Mini Warm-up

L.H. R.H.

Norwegian Folk Tune

Andante

p

MORE ABOUT RESTS

What kind of Rest is this?

What kind of Rest is this?

What kind of Rest is this?

Here is a Quaver (♪) Rest.

It is very short!

½ of a 𝄽

call that a rest?

Draw 3 ♪ Rests

Play this rhythm on any note with finger **3** of your

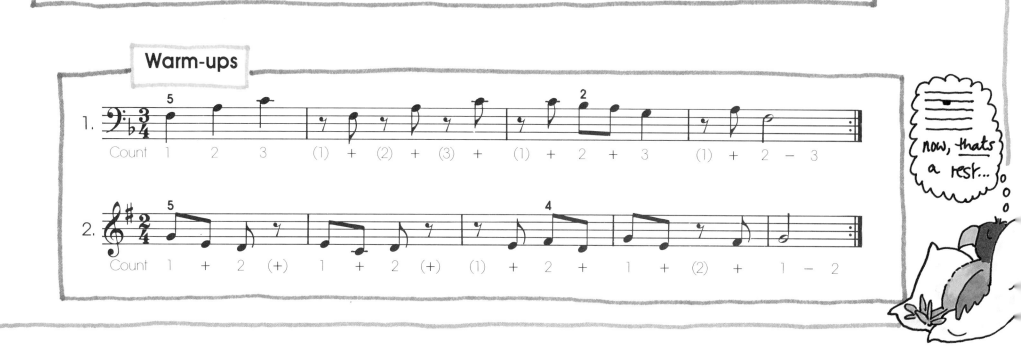

Warm-ups

now, thats a rest...

ERIC TAKES A BREATHER

Look carefully at the hand positions before you start:

Supplementary material: Warm Up With Chester Part One, p.19. Chester's Music Puzzles Set Two, paper 8.

CAT'S CRADLE

If there are four ♪s in a **2/4** Bar, they are often grouped like this:

Sometimes they are grouped like this in a Bar of **4/4**, if the first two or last two beats are ♪s.  ✓

but not  ✗

Cat's Cradle is a game played with a piece of string by two children.
It used to be very popular in England.

ECOSSAISE

A popular type of ballroom dance in Weber's time.

= Stress the note.

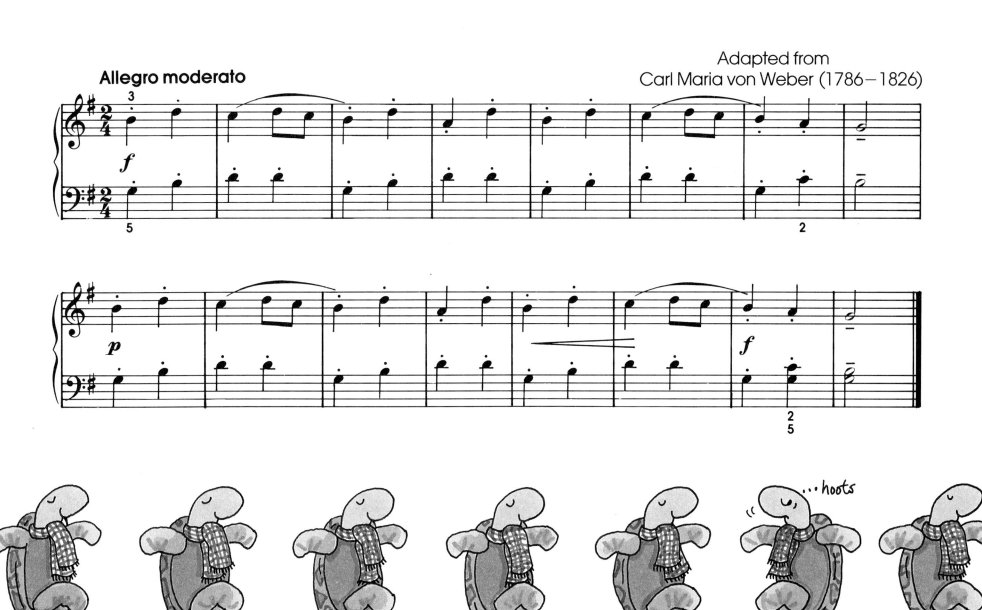

Allegro moderato

Adapted from
Carl Maria von Weber (1786–1826)

...hoots

FREE POSITIONS

Set 5-finger hand positions will not necessarily be used from now on:

Make sure you know these notes:

 and

B C D E F G A B C D E F   C D E F G A B C D

Always look carefully at the first note of each Phrase or section to work out where you should be playing. You may need to stretch your hand or jump more than 5 notes from now on.   Feel free!

Warm-ups

1.

2.

3.

4.

Copy Warm-ups 2. and 3. into your Manuscript Book and add the letter-names.

GREEN WILLOW

This piece includes all the notes you have learnt in the .
Make sure you use the correct fingering.
Move carefully from one short Phrase to another.
Moving to different places is called the 'geography' of the keyboard.

Supplementary material:
Warm Up With Chester Part One, p.20.
Chester's Piano Starters Volume Two, p.9.

SKIP TO MY LOU

Second Player

Play the music on this page an Octave **lower** than it is written.

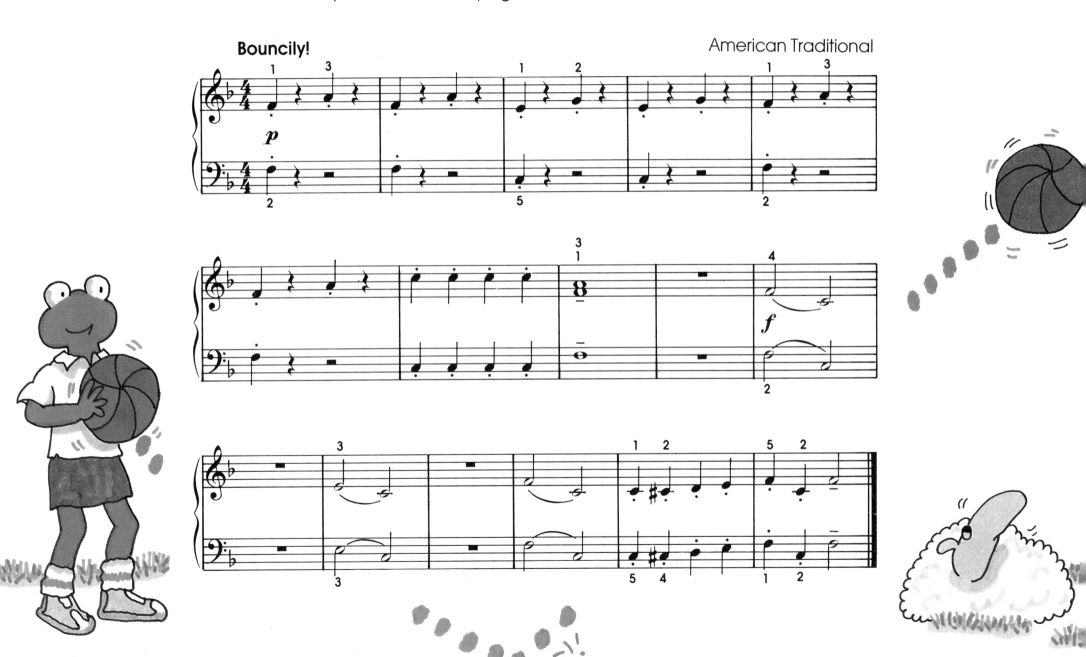

Bouncily!

American Traditional

BOUNCE!!

DUET

SKIP TO MY LOU

First Player

Play the music on this page an Octave **higher** than it is written.

CHORALE

When you play this famous old tune in your , listen to the sound you are
making and try to produce a beautiful singing tone.
Get used to the 'geography' of the keyboard.

Adagio

An Old German Hymn

MY HAT, IT HAS THREE CORNERS!

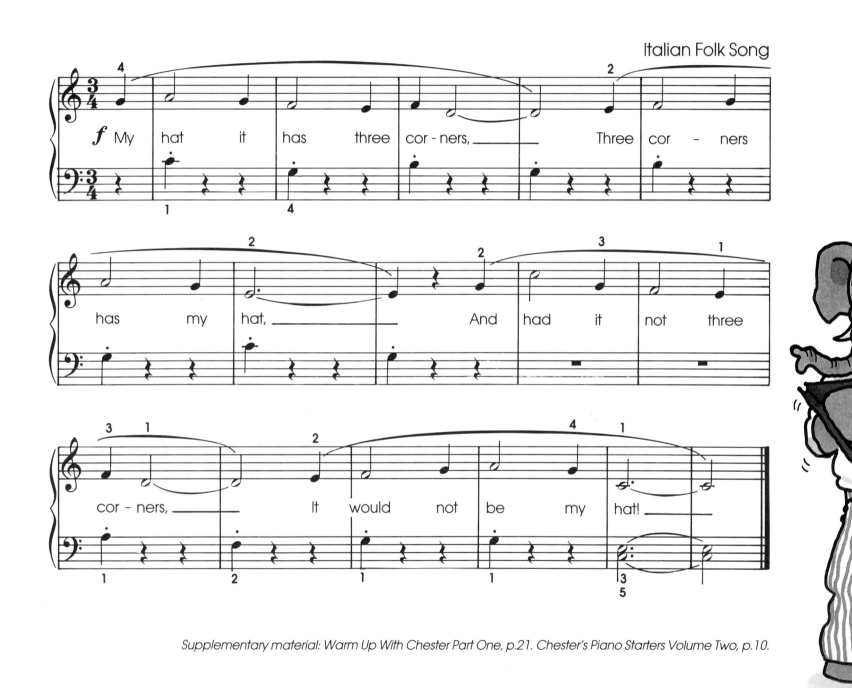

Italian Folk Song

Supplementary material: Warm Up With Chester Part One, p.21. Chester's Piano Starters Volume Two, p.10.

A LITTLE TUNE

pp (**pianissimo**) = Very soft   **mp** (**mezzo piano**) = Moderately soft

ff (**fortissimo**) = Very loud   **mf** (**mezzo forte**) = Moderately loud

Dmitri Kabalevsky (1904—1987)

Watch Out!
In both these tunes
both hands are in the 𝄞.

We're giving
absolutely no
clues

HUNT THE TUNE!

When you know what the tune is, find and play the rest of it in the
and write this L.H. tune in full in your Manuscript Book.

Four Bars of a Nursery Rhyme

and so on!

MO IN MOSCOW

accel. (accelerando) = Get faster

Russian Folk Tune

Supplementary material: Chester's Piano Starters Volume Two, p.11.

TIED QUAVERS

Tap out this rhythm on your knee.
Nod your head on the tied Quavers where you see the circled counts.

Count 1 + 2 + 1 + ②+ 1 + ②+ 1 + 2

Play the rhythms below on one note — make sure you don't actually play the tied ♪s.
The circles have been added to help you.

Count 1 + ②+ 3 4 1 + ②+ 3 + ④+ 1 – 2 3 – 4

Say the words as you play this one.

Brad·ley_ the e - le-phant likes pack-ing_ his trunk for the ho - li - days.

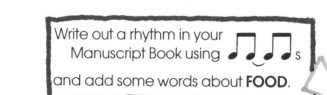

Write out a rhythm in your
Manuscript Book using ♪♪♪s
and add some words about **FOOD**.

Warm-up

PORRIDGE AND ONIONS!

Before you play this piece, 1) Say it in rhythm 2) Clap it

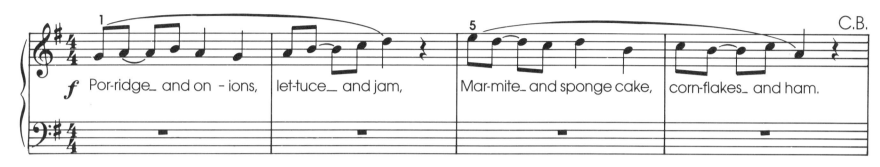

C.B.

f Por-ridge and on - ions, let-tuce and jam, Mar-mite and sponge cake, corn-flakes and ham.

Ba-con and ho - ney, tof-fee and cress. Stir them all to-ge-ther. Ugh! what a mess.

YOGHURT AND TURNIPS!

C.B.

Supplementary material: Chester's Music Puzzles Set Two, paper 9.

LIZZIE'S CAKE—WALK

In Bar 7 move your hand **towards** the black key (C♯) when you bounce off the **D** in Bar 6.

Supplementary material: Warm Up With Chester Part One, p.22.

OLD DAN TUCKER

FINGERS—OVER—THUMBS

For this trick I will need 6 notes and 5 fingers....

This will give you 6 notes without moving from a 5-note hand position.

Put finger **1** of your ✋ on **G**.
Now move finger **2** over this thumb and play **A**.
Then play **G** with **1** again.
Play these notes with this fingering several times

‖: 1 2 1 2 :‖
G A G A

Put finger **1** of your ✋ on **D**.
Now move finger **2** over this thumb and play **C**.
Then play **D** with **1** again.
Play these notes with this fingering several times

‖: 1 2 1 2 :‖
D C D C

In your Manuscript Book write 4 Bars of music for the ✋ using these notes:

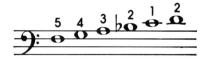

Warm-ups

6 notes with 5 fingers without moving out of position!

Fingers-over-thumbs = F—O—T

For this trick I will need 6 chocolates and 5 seconds

THE WOODPECKER

Mini Warm-up

Can you hear any pecking?

German Folk Tune

Supplementary material: Warm Up With Chester Part One, p.23. Chester's Piano Starters Volume Two, p.12.

CRUISING

Watch out — the Time Signature keeps changing.

THE CAT

(from *Peter and the Wolf*)

This is a real test of your keyboard 'geography'!
In the story, the cat is prowling towards the bird when you hear this tune.

Adapted from
Serge Prokofiev (1891 – 1953)

Supplementary material: Chester's Piano Starters Volume Two, p.13.

HOLIDAY TIME

For the Repeat, try playing both hands an Octave higher than they are written.
Watch out for fingers-over-thumbs in the

THE CRANES ARE FLYING

(Ukranian Folk Song)

Look carefully at the Clefs on this page.

Moderato

Anton Arensky (1861 – 1906)

THE PARROT IS PECKING!

Crossly!

C.B.

DOTTED CROTCHETS

A dot after a note makes it longer by one half of itself.

$\text{♩.} = \text{♩} + \text{♪}$ (Think of ♩. ♪ as ♩▭♫)

Hold on to the dot — it is half a count. The other half of the count could be ♪ or 𝄾

Two examples:

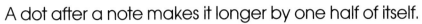

2/4 ♩.   ♪ | ♩.   𝄾 ‖   **4/4** ♩.   ♪ ♩ ♩ | ♩ ♩.   ♪ ♩ ‖

1 – 2 + 1 – 2 (+)   1 – 2 + 3   4   1   2 – 3 + 4

Clap this rhythm:

3/4 ♩.   ♪ ♪ | ♩   ♩ | ♩.   ♪ ♪ | ♩ | ♩.   ♪ ♪ | ♩   ♩ | ♩.   ♪ ♪ | ♩.   ‖

1 – 2 + 3   1 – 2   3   1 – 2 + 3   1 – 2 – 3   1 – 2 + 3   1 – 2   3   1 – 2 + 3   1 – 2 – 3

It is the rhythm of the first 8 Bars of *Rock-a-Bye Baby*.

Now play this Nursery Rhyme as a Warm-up.

Warm-up

TWO THEMES BY MOZART

Adapted from
Wolfgang Amadeus Mozart
(1756–1791)

1. A Song from an Opera
   called *Don Giovanni*

2. From a Piano Sonata

Remember — miss out
the 1X (first time Bar)
when you repeat
the music.

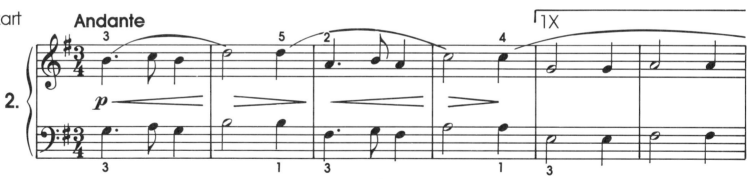

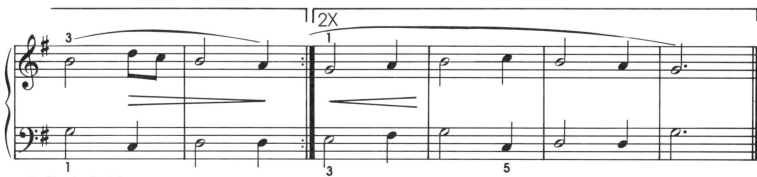

Supplementary material: Warm Up With Chester Part One, p.24. Chester's Piano Starters Volume Two, p.14. Chester's Music Puzzles Set 2, paper 10.

42

TURKEY IN THE STRAW

(He is getting quite old by now!)

American Traditional

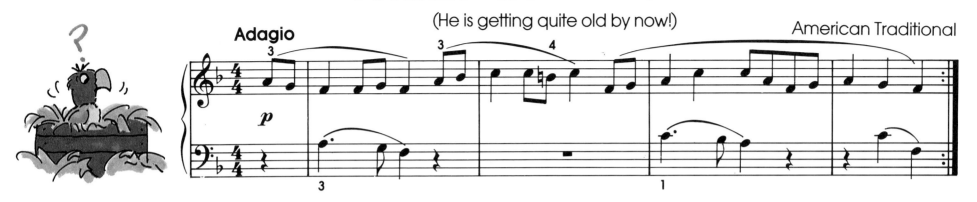

CANON

Do you remember what a Canon is?

Before you play:

1) Clap the 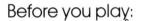 rhythm of the first 4 Bars.

2) Tap out the rhythm on your right knee, and the rhythm on your left knee, at the same time.

3) Look carefully at the Phrase-Marks.
   The sign // has been added in this piece, to remind you when to lift each hand off.

K. Künz (1812–1875)

SUSY, LITTLE SUSY

Humperdinck used this German Folk Tune in his Opera *Hansel and Gretel.*

Adapted from
Engelbert Humperdinck (1854 – 1921)

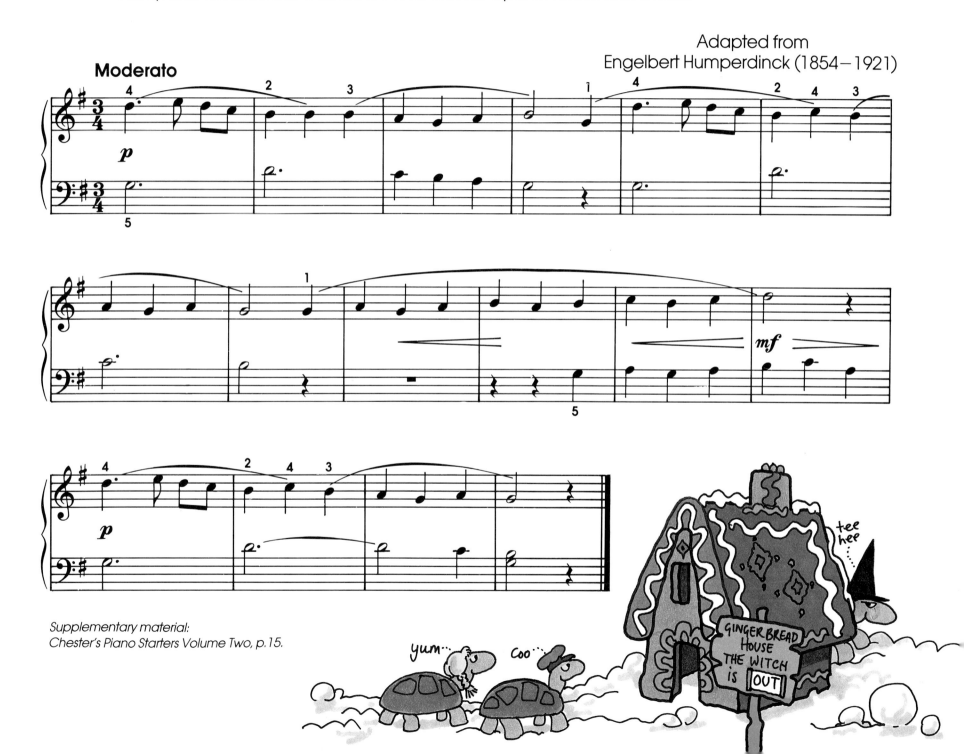

Supplementary material:
Chester's Piano Starters Volume Two, p.15.

SHEPHERD'S HEY

The 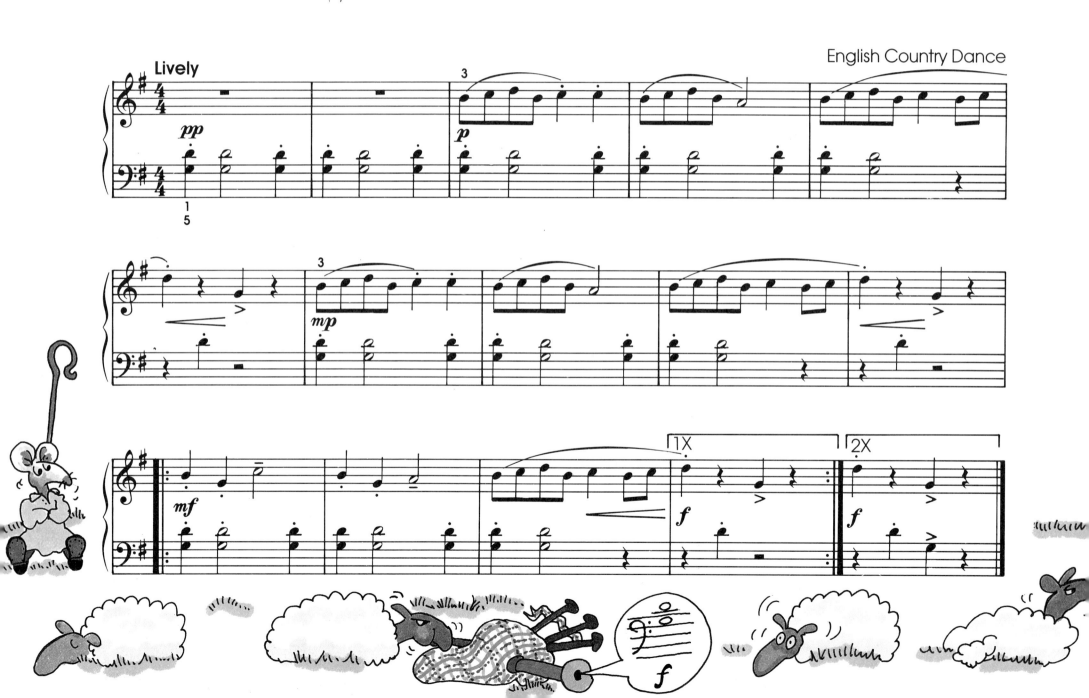 in this piece has a Drone Bass to make it sound like Bagpipes.

English Country Dance

ECOSSAISE

Mini Warm-up

This piece is in a Minor Key — **A** Minor.

Watch out — the 🖐 visits the Treble Clef in Bars 9—12.

Adapted from
Franz Schubert (1797—1828)

Allegro moderato

JUNIOR'S JIVE

A New Key Signature (2♭s) — All the **B**s and **E**s are **B**♭s and **E**♭s.

Watch out for the Accidentals in this piece — **C**♯s, **G**♯s, and **F**♯s.
In this style of music (blues, rags etc.) there will always be quite a few Accidentals.
Remember to move your hand **towards** the black keys.

C.B.

Supplementary material: Chester's Piano Starters Volume Two, p.16.

Having finished this book, the pupil may now move on to the following:

Chester's Piano Book Number Three (CH 55128)
(The tutor is part of the series called **Chester's Piano Books**,
and follows on from Book Three of *this* series.)

Chester's Piano Starters Volume Three (CH 55663)
Warm Up With Chester Part Two (CH 55806)
Chester's Music Puzzles Set Three (CH 55833)

TRUE OR FALSE? Book 2   Answers: 1. ✗ 2. ✗ 3. ✓ 4. ✗ 5. ✓ 6. ✗ 7. ✓ 8. ✓ 9. ✗ 10. ✓
11. ✗ 12. ✓ 13. ✓ 14. ✗ 15. ✗ 16. ✗ 17. ✓ 18. ✗ 19. ✓ 20. ✗

TRUE OR FALSE?

Put ✓ for True and ✗ for False.

1. 𝄐 = Pause.

2. rit. = Get faster.

3. 🎼♭ = Key Signature of **G** Major.

4. 𝄽 = ♪ Rest

5. accel. = Slow down.

6. *mf* = Very loud.

7. Adagio = Slow.

8. 🎼 = **F.**

9. ♩. = Staccato.

10. 𝄢♯ = Key Signature of **G** Major.

11. *pp* = Very soft.

12. ♩ = Accent.

13. Ecossaise = a March.

14. A tempo = Back to the original speed.

15. 𝄢 𝅝 𝅝 = A 4th.

16. ♩. = ♩ + ♪

17. Andante = Fast.

18. ♫♫ = ♬♬

19. *mp* = Moderately soft.

20. 🎼♭ = Key Signature of **F** Major.

The answers are overleaf.

Certificate

This is to certify that ....

....

has successfully completed Book 3 of Chester's Easiest Piano Course,

CONGRATULATIONS!

Signed (teacher) ....

Date ....